Walt Disney's

Bambi & the Butterfly

A GOLDEN BOOK • NEW YORK
Western Publishing Company, Inc., Racine, Wisconsin 53404

One morning Thumper hopped into Bambi's thicket home.

"Hi, Bambi!" he said. "Do you want to go down to the stream to play?"

"May I?" Bambi asked his mother. "Yes, Bambi, but be careful in the forest," his mother said.

On the way, Bambi and Thumper
saw Flower, the skunk. "Would you
like to come to the stream?"
asked Bambi.

"No, thanks," said Flower.
"I'm sleepy and anyway it
looks like rain."

Bambi and Thumper saw some
opossums hanging upside-down
by their tails.

"Hello, opossums," said Bambi.

"Hello," said the opossums.

Bambi ran ahead and poked
his nose in a bush. He was looking
for sweet berries, but he found
something else instead.

"What are you looking at?"
asked Thumper.
"I don't know," said Bambi.
"Come and see."

Thumper poked his nose in the bush, too. "I see a chrysalis," he said. "Soon a butterfly will come out. But we don't know when, so let's keep on going."

On their way to the stream,
they saw Owl flying overhead.
"Hello, Owl. Where are you
going?" called Bambi.

"Home to my nest,"
Owl called back.
"See you tomorrow."

When they got to the stream,
Bambi and Thumper said
hello to the ducks —

and to the big green frog
who went *plop! splash!*
into the water.

They said hello to a raccoon who
was washing his food in the water.

Bambi leaped across the stream.
"That was a good jump, Bambi!"
said Thumper.
Bambi jumped
back again.

Suddenly the sky grew darker.
Rain started to fall. Everyone ran
for cover.

It rained and rained.
When the storm ended, Bambi
asked Thumper, "Do you think
the chrysalis is all right?"
"Let's hurry back and look,"
Thumper said.

Thumper was the first to look
in the bush.
"Bambi! Come here!"
he called.

Bambi poked his nose
in the bush....
"Hello, butterfly," he said.